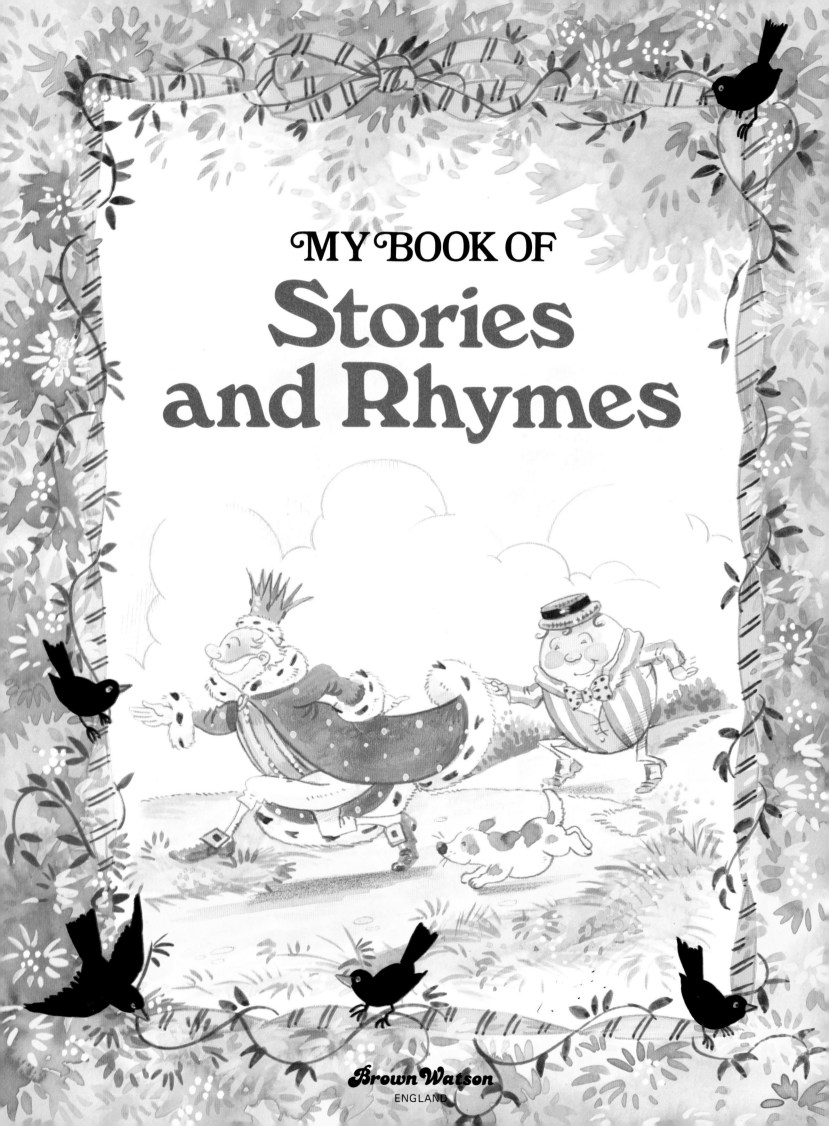

MY BOOK OF
Stories
and Rhymes

Brown Watson
ENGLAND

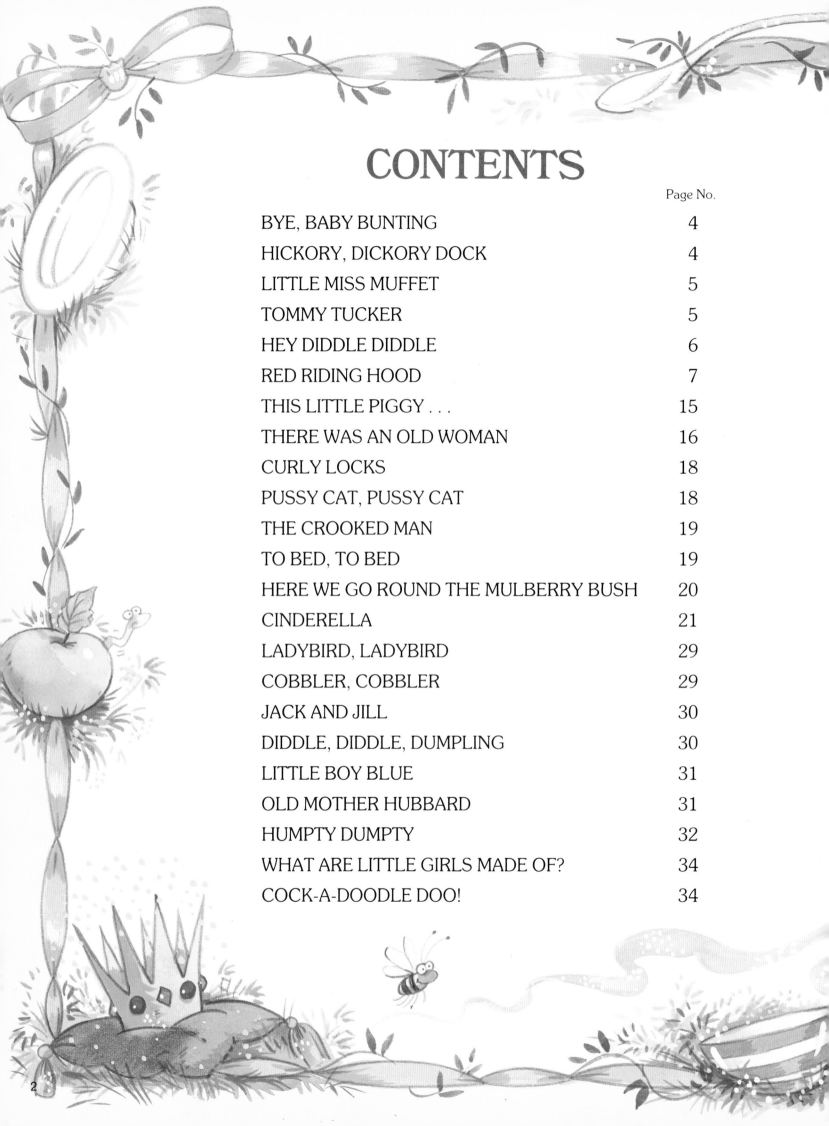

CONTENTS

BYE, BABY BUNTING

Bye, Baby Bunting,
Daddy's gone a-hunting,
Gone to get a rabbit skin
To wrap the Baby Bunting in.

HICKORY, DICKORY DOCK

Hickory, dickory dock,
The mouse ran up the clock.
The clock struck one,
The mouse ran down,
Hickory, dickory dock.

LITTLE MISS MUFFET

Little Miss Muffet
Sat on a tuffet,
Eating her curds and whey;
There came a big spider,
Who sat down beside her
And frightened Miss Muffet away.

TOMMY TUCKER

Little Tommy Tucker sang for his supper;
What shall we give him?
White bread and butter.
How shall he cut it without any knife?
How will he marry, without any wife?

5

HEY DIDDLE DIDDLE

Hey diddle, diddle
The cat and the fiddle,
The cow jumped over the moon;
The little dog laughed
To see such sport,
And the dish ran away with the spoon.

RED RIDING HOOD

One morning Little Red Riding Hood's mother asked her to take a basket of food to her Grandma who was in bed and not feeling very well. "Do go straight to Grandma's house," said her mother and dressed her in her red cape and hood.

On her way through the wood, Little Red Riding Hood met a wolf who asked her where she was going. "To see my Grandma who is ill in bed," said Little Red Riding Hood.

"Where does she live?" asked the wolf. "At the cottage in the wood," said Little Red Riding Hood without thinking, and before she knew what had happened the wolf turned and ran off.

The wolf rushed straight to the cottage where Grandma lived and when he arrived he knocked at the door. "Who is there?" called Grandma, and the wolf replied, "It's Little Red Riding Hood, Grandma." "Lift the latch and come in," said Grandma. When she saw the wolf she was so frightened, she hid herself in the cupboard.

The wolf quickly put on Grandma's bed-cap and waited for Little Red Riding Hood to arrive. "Who is there?" he called in a voice like Grandma's when he heard her knock. "It is Little Red Riding Hood," she answered. "Lift the latch and come in," said the wolf.

"How are you feeling?" said Little Red Riding Hood. "Much better thank you dear," said the wolf and as he spoke, his bed cap slipped from his head so that Little Red Riding Hood could see his ears. "What big ears you have!" said Little Red Riding Hood nervously. "All the better to hear you with," said the wolf.

"What big teeth you have," cried Little Red Riding Hood. "All the better to eat you with," shouted the wolf as he jumped out of the bed. "You are not my Grandma!" screamed Little Red Riding Hood. "No, I am the big bad wolf, and I am going to eat you up!"

As Little Red Riding Hood ran from the house, a woodcutter who was cutting some trees outside heard her cries for help. He chased the wolf down the path and the wolf ran off into the woods as fast as he could.

The woodcutter took Little Red Riding Hood back into the cottage to see if the nasty wolf had eaten her Grandma. As they called her, a voice said, "I am in the cupboard, is it safe to come out?" When Grandma heard Little Red Riding Hood's voice she knew that all was well.

"How lucky we both are to be safe!" said Little Red Riding Hood as she hugged her Grandma.

They both thanked the woodcutter and asked him to stay for tea.

THIS LITTLE PIGGY . . .

This little piggy went to market.
This little piggy stayed at home.
This little piggy had roast beef.
This little piggy had none.
And this little piggy cried,
"Wee-wee-wee,"
All the way home.

THERE WAS AN OLD WOMAN

There was an old woman,
Who lived in a shoe,
She had so many children
She didn't know what to do;
She gave them some broth,
Without any bread,
She whipped them all soundly,
And sent them to bed.

CURLY LOCKS

Curly Locks, Curly Locks, will you be mine?
You shall not wash dishes, nor yet feed the swine;
You'll sit on a cushion and sew a fine seam,
And feed upon strawberries, sugar and cream.

PUSSY CAT, PUSSY CAT

Pussy cat, pussy cat,
Where have you been?
I've been up to London,
To visit the Queen.

Pussy cat, pussy cat,
What did you there?
I frightened a little mouse,
'Neath the Queen's chair.

18

THE CROOKED MAN

There was a crooked man,
And he walked a crooked mile.
He found a crooked sixpence
Beside a crooked stile;

He bought a crooked cat,
Which caught a crooked mouse,
And they all lived together
In a little crooked house.

TO BED, TO BED

"To bed, to bed!" said Sleepy Head.
"Tarry a while," said Slow.
"Put on the pan," said greedy Ann.
"We'll sup before we go."

HERE WE GO ROUND THE MULBERRY BUSH

Here we go round the mulberry bush,
The mulberry bush, the mulberry bush,
Here we go round the mulberry bush,
On a cold and frosty morning.

CINDERELLA

Cinderella lived in a big house with her father and two stepsisters. The stepsisters were very unkind to her and made her do all the housework. Although she was pretty they made her dress in rags instead of nice clothes.

Cinderella's stepsisters spent most of their time in front of the mirror powdering their noses and making Cinderella brush their hair.

One day an invitation to the ball
arrived from the palace.
"May I go?" asked Cinderella.

Cinderella's stepsisters
laughed and said that it was
impossible. This made
Cinderella very sad. When
her stepsisters finally left for
the ball, Cinderella sat
crying by the fire.

Cinderella was quite alone in the house, and was surprised to hear a voice saying, "I am your Fairy Godmother, and you shall go to the ball. Bring me a pumpkin, four white mice and three lizards."

As fast as lightning, the pumpkin was changed into a coach, the four white mice into four lovely white horses and the lizards into a coach driver and two footmen.

When the Fairy Godmother waved her wand, Cinderella's rags changed into a wonderful ball dress and she had dainty glass slippers on her feet. "You must leave the palace before twelve o' clock, or everything will change back to how it was before," her Fairy Godmother told her.

Cinderella so enjoyed dancing with the Prince that she forgot the time and soon the clock struck twelve. She ran quickly down the palace steps. As she ran, the Prince tried to stop her, but she was gone.

The Prince found one of Cinderella's tiny glass slippers and told his footmen, "I will marry the girl whose foot it will fit!"

The footmen travelled for many miles in search of the owner, and, on their way back to the palace, they called at Cinderella's house. The two stepsisters tried to make the slipper fit them, but it was no use.

Just as they were leaving, Cinderella's father said that she should be allowed to try the slipper. It fitted her perfectly. Cinderella married the Prince and became the happiest girl in the land.

LADYBIRD, LADYBIRD

Ladybird, ladybird,
Fly away home,
Your house is on fire
And your children all gone;
All except one,
And that's little Ann,
And she crept under
The warming pan.

COBBLER, COBBLER

Cobbler, cobbler, mend my shoe,
Get it done by half-past-two;
Stitch it up and stitch it down,
Then I'll give you half-a-crown.

JACK AND JILL

Jack and Jill went up the hill,
To fetch a pail of water;
Jack fell down, and broke his crown,
And Jill came tumbling after.

DIDDLE, DIDDLE, DUMPLING

Diddle, diddle, dumpling, my son John,
Went to bed with his trousers on;
One shoe off and one shoe on,
Diddle, diddle, dumpling, my son John.

LITTLE BOY BLUE

Little Boy Blue,
Come blow your horn;
The sheep's in the meadow,
The cow's in the corn.

Where is the boy
Who looks after the sheep?
He's under the haystack,
Fast asleep.

OLD MOTHER HUBBARD

Old Mother Hubbard
Went to the cupboard,
To get her poor doggy a bone;
But when she got there,
The cupboard was bare,
And so the poor doggy got none!

31

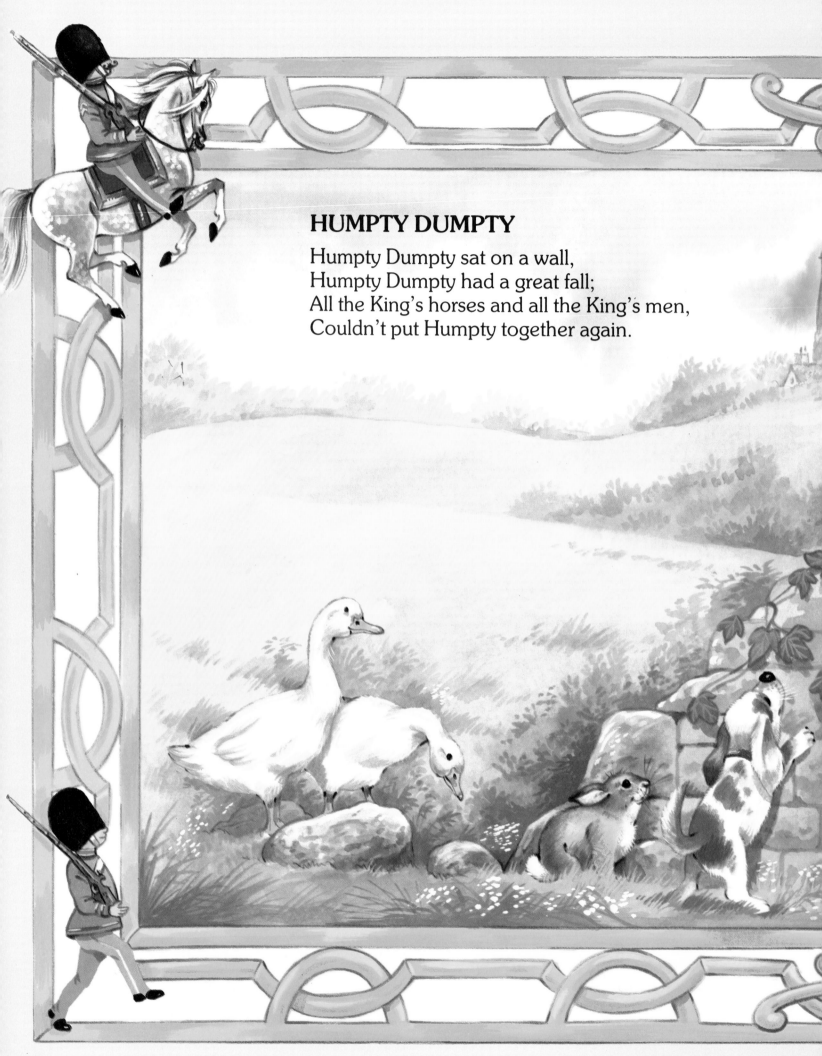

HUMPTY DUMPTY

Humpty Dumpty sat on a wall,
Humpty Dumpty had a great fall;
All the King's horses and all the King's men,
Couldn't put Humpty together again.

WHAT ARE LITTLE GIRLS MADE OF?

What are little girls made of, made of?
What are little girls made of?
Sugar and spice,
And all things nice,
That's what little girls are made of.

What are little boys made of, made of?
What are little boys made of?
Snips and snails,
And puppy dogs' tails,
That's what little boys
are made of.

COCK-A-DOODLE DOO!

Cock-a-doodle doo!
My dame has lost her shoe,
My master's lost his fiddling stick,
And knows not what to do.

LITTLE BO-PEEP

Little Bo-peep has lost her sheep,
And doesn't know where to find them;
Leave them alone, and they'll come home,
Bringing their tails behind them.

JACK BE NIMBLE

Jack be nimble,
Jack be quick,
Jack jump over
The candlestick.

RING-A-RING O' ROSES

Ring-a-ring o' roses,
A pocket full of posies,
A-tishoo! A-tishoo!
We all fall down.

SLEEPING BEAUTY

Many years ago a King and Queen told everyone of the birth of their baby. The fairies in the land brought the baby gifts, but one wicked fairy promised that when the Princess was fifteen years old, she would prick her finger and go to sleep for one hundred years.

On her fifteenth birthday, the Princess took a walk through her castle and found a room where an old woman sat spinning. "Will you show me how to spin?" the Princess asked.

The old woman showed her what to do but when she touched the needle she pricked her finger and fell asleep at once, and so did everyone else in the castle.

Years passed and one day a handsome Prince was riding by the castle and decided to take a look inside. He was surprised to find that everyone was asleep.

Soon he found the Princess and thought how beautiful she was. He knelt down by her side and kissed her.

At that moment the spell was broken and the Princess and all the other people in the castle woke up from their deep sleep.

The Princess told the Prince
the story of the wicked
fairy's spell and how she
had pricked her finger.

Soon the Prince and the
Princess fell in love with each
other and decided to marry.

The King and Queen arranged a lovely wedding for their daughter and her Prince and all the townsfolk and servants in the castle danced and danced until the next morning.

The Prince and Princess and everyone in the castle lived happily ever after.

MARY, MARY

Mary, Mary, quite contrary,
How does your garden grow?
With silver bells and cockle shells,
And pretty maids all in a row.

LITTLE JACK HORNER

Little Jack Horner sat in the corner,
Eating a Christmas pie;
He put in his thumb,
And pulled out a plum,
And said, "What a good boy am I!"

GOOSEY GANDER

Goosey, goosey gander,
Where do you wander?
Upstairs and downstairs,
And in my lady's chamber,
Where I met an old man,
Who wouldn't say his prayers–
I took him by the left leg,
And threw him down the stairs.

GEORGIE PORGIE

Georgie Porgie, pudding and pie,
Kissed the girls and made them cry;
When the boys came out to play,
Georgie Porgie ran away.

ROCK-A-BYE BABY

Rock-a-bye baby,
On a tree-top,
When the wind blows
The cradle will rock.

When the bough breaks,
The cradle will fall –
Down will come baby,
Cradle and all!

TOM THE PIPER'S SON

Tom, Tom, the piper's son,
Stole a pig and away did run;
The pig was eat,
And Tom was beat,
And Tom went howling down the street.

BOYS AND GIRLS COME OUT TO PLAY!

Boys and girls come out to play,
The moon does shine as bright as day.
Leave your supper and leave your sleep,
And join your friends out in the street.
Come with a whoop and come with a call,
Come with good will or not at all.
Up the ladder and down the wall,
A half-penny loaf will serve us all;
You find milk and I'll find flour,
And we'll have a pudding in half-an-hour.

WEE WILLIE WINKIE

Wee Willie Winkie
Runs through the town,
Upstairs and downstairs
In his nightgown;
Rapping at the window,
Crying through the lock,
Are the children all in bed,
For now it's eight o'clock.

POLLY FLINDERS

Little Polly Flinders
Sat among the cinders,
Warming her pretty little toes;
Her mother came and caught her,
And smacked her little daughter,
For spoiling her nice new clothes.

MARY HAD A LITTLE LAMB

Mary had a little lamb,
Its fleece was white as snow,
And everywhere that Mary went
That lamb was sure to go.

It followed her to school one day–
That was against the rule;
It made the children laugh and play,
To see a lamb at school.

SEE-SAW MARGERY DAW

See-saw Margery Daw,
Jack shall have a new master;
Jack shall work for a penny a day,
Because he can't work any faster.

RIDE A COCK-HORSE TO BANBURY CROSS

Ride a cock-horse to Banbury Cross,
To see a fine lady upon a white horse;
Rings on her fingers and bells on her toes,
She shall have music wherever she goes.

JACK SPRAT COULD EAT NO FAT

Jack Sprat could eat no fat,
His wife could eat no lean,
So it came to pass, between them both,
They licked the platter clean.

Jack ate all the lean,
Joan ate all the fat,
The bone they picked it clean,
Then gave it to the cat.

THERE WAS A LITTLE GIRL

There was a little girl and she had a little curl,
Right in the middle of her forehead;
When she was good, she was very, very good,
But when she was bad, she was horrid!

SIMPLE SIMON

Simple Simon met a pieman,
Going to the fair;
Said Simple Simon to the pieman:
"Let me taste your ware."
Said the pieman to Simple Simon:
"Show me first your penny."
Said Simple Simon to the pieman:
"Indeed, I have not any."

POLLY PUT THE KETTLE ON

Polly put the kettle on,
Polly put the kettle on,
Polly put the kettle on,
We'll all have tea.

Sukey take it off again,
Sukey take it off again,
Sukey take it off again,
They've all gone home.

THREE BLIND MICE

Three blind mice, three blind mice,
See how they run, see how they run!
They all ran after the farmer's wife,
Who cut off their tails with the carving knife,
Did you ever see such a thing in your life,
As three blind mice?